Dear Parent:
Your child's love of reading starts here!

Every child learns to read in a different way and at his or her own speed. Some go back and forth between reading levels and read favorite books again and again. Others read through each level in order. You can help your young reader improve and become more confident by encouraging his or her own interests and abilities. From books your child reads with you to the first books he or she reads alone, there are I Can Read Books for every stage of reading:

SHARED READING
Basic language, word repetition, and whimsical illustrations, ideal for sharing with your emergent reader

BEGINNING READING
Short sentences, familiar words, and simple concepts for children eager to read on their own

READING WITH HELP
Engaging stories, longer sentences, and language play for developing readers

READING ALONE
Complex plots, challenging vocabulary, and high-interest topics for the independent reader

I Can Read Books have introduced children to the joy of reading since 1957. Featuring award-winning authors and illustrators and a fabulous cast of beloved characters, I Can Read Books set the standard for beginning readers.

A lifetime of discovery begins with the magical words **"I Can Read!"**

Visit www.icanread.com for information on enriching your child's reading experience.

To children everywhere, use your voice and remember
the words of the great Fannie Lou Hamer:
"Nobody's free until everybody's free."
—A.D.

For Mom
—K.M.

I Can Read® and I Can Read Book® are trademarks of HarperCollins Publishers.

Freedom Celebration: A Juneteenth Party
Text copyright © 2025 by Angela Dalton
Illustration copyright © 2025 by Keisha Morris
All rights reserved. Manufactured in Johor, Malaysia.
No part of this book may be used or reproduced in any manner whatsoever without written permission except in the case of brief quotations embodied in critical articles and reviews. For information address HarperCollins Children's Books, a division of HarperCollins Publishers, 195 Broadway, New York, NY 10007.
www.icanread.com

Library of Congress Control Number: 2024945851
ISBN 978-0-06-333497-7 (trade bdg.) — ISBN 978-0-06-333495-3 (pbk.)

The artist used collaged tissue paper in photoshop to create the digital illustrations for this book.
Book design by Elaine Lopez

25 26 27 28 29   PCA   10 9 8 7 6 5 4 3 2 1   First Edition

FREEDOM CELEBRATION

A Juneteenth Party

BY ANGELA DALTON
ART BY KEISHA MORRIS

HARPER
An Imprint of HarperCollinsPublishers

Hi, friend! Good to see you.
I'm glad you came
to my family barbecue.
Today we're celebrating
a very important day.

The Morris family has honored this holiday for a real long time.

Do you know what it is?
It's called Juneteenth,
and it's a freedom celebration!

Now, you might be thinking, "What's Juneteenth?"
Well, grab a plate and I'll tell you!
Juneteenth is a combination of the words *June* and *nineteenth*.

Juneteenth is also called
Freedom Day or Jubilee Day.
It honors the date June 19, 1865.
Isn't that right, Grandma Daisy?

"It sure is, Gloria. But the Juneteenth story starts before that.

More than three hundred years ago, European enslavers kidnapped African people from their homes. They brought them to this country and forced them to work without pay and to live with no freedom."

"It's called slavery,
and it was a shameful time in our country.
Anyone with sense knew it was wrong.

Enslavers bought and sold African people,
separating them from their families.
African people fought
for their freedom many times.
But slave owners created laws
called slave codes that kept them enslaved."

My cousins and I made these posters
to show our love for all the people
in our family tree.
Because of them,
we are here together today.

"Those posters are beautiful, Gloria. Now, what was I saying? Oh yes! Southerners made lots of money from slavery, and some folks in the North didn't like that.

Newly elected President Lincoln wanted to stop slavery from spreading to the West. Angry Southerners threatened to separate from the United States. Slavery divided the United States so much that on April 12, 1861, the Civil War began."

Some Black people found ways to escape
the South to fight with the North.
They did this to fight for their freedom.
There was a lot of bloodshed and lives lost.
That's why we eat food that is red,
like red velvet cake,
and drink red drinks, like strawberry punch,
for Juneteenth.

President Lincoln needed
more people to fight in the war.
So he signed—
uh, what do you call it, Uncle Fred?

"The Emancipation Proclamation.
Sound it out with me now:
e-man-suh-pay-shun prah-cluh-may-shun.
There ya go!
He signed it on January 1, 1863.

This allowed more people to fight,
but it only freed some Black people
in some Southern states.
So he signed the Thirteenth Amendment,
ending slavery.
Now the North had more men,
both Black and white,
fighting against the South together."

Most of the Black people
who were still enslaved
heard the news that they were free.
But those in Texas weren't told the news.

It took a whole two years,
five months, and eighteen days
for their freedom to arrive!

"You know your history, lil' Glo!
Why it took so long, no one knows.
Some say Texas enslavers
ignored the president's orders
and forced people to keep working.

What we do know is that two years after slavery became illegal, Union general Gordon Granger arrived in Galveston, Texas."

On June 19, the general rode into town with white and Black soldiers and read General Order Number Three. It said everyone was free.

Today, we celebrate with
Freedom Day parades.
We sing songs like
"Lift Every Voice and Sing."
This day reminds us of the struggles
Black people have gone through,
and still go through,
to fight for their freedom.

I'm glad that you came to honor this holiday with us. Juneteenth is a special celebration for my family.

This day reminds us that
Black people are strong people.
That we're intelligent people.
That our history is American history.

On this day . . .
we honor the people lost during slavery,
we gather with those who survived,
and we remember that it's important
to fight for freedom for everyone.

No one is free until we're all free.
Happy Juneteenth!

AUTHOR'S NOTE

The story of Juneteenth is hard to explain for many reasons. For generations, Black Americans were not seen as human by many white people. And so, our history was erased, changed, or ignored. Also, the Civil War is complicated. Historians struggle to understand its beginnings to this very day. What we do know is that it started because of power and money. The South benefited from having enslaved people work their fields for free, and people in the North were upset by the profit Southerners made doing so. Many historians believe that both the war and Lincoln's politics used Black people's lives like pawns in a game of chess.

Though this form of slavery did end, the fight for freedom continues in the United States. It's important that everyone celebrate this holiday because it is a right we all deserve. As the famous Black leader Fannie Lou Hamer once said, "Nobody's free until everybody's free."

—ANGELA DALTON